Dora's Big Dig

by Alison Inches
illustrated by Robert Roper

SIMON AND SCHUSTER/NICKELODEON

Based on the TV series *Dora the Explorer* as seen on Nick Jr.

SIMON AND SCHUSTER
First published in Great Britain in 2007 by Simon & Schuster UK Ltd
Africa House, 64-78 Kingsway, London WC2B 6AH
A CBS COMPANY

Originally published in the USA in 2006 by Simon Spotlight,
an imprint of Simon & Schuster Children's Division, New York.

A CIP catalogue record for this book is available from the British Library

ISBN -10: 1847380476
ISBN - 13: 9781847380470
Printed in China

10 9 8 7 6 5 4 3 2 1

Visit our websites: www.simonsays.co.uk
www.nickjr.co.uk

¡Hola! I'm Dora, and today I'm digging in the garden.
Dig! Dig! Dig!

Wow! I've uncovered a turquoise stone. Ooooh, maybe this is an ancient treasure!

I should take this stone to my *mami*. My *mami* is an archeologist. That means she digs for ancient treasure! She'll know what to do with an ancient treasure.

First I need to pick up my friend Boots.

Look, Boots! The stone has a jaguar's face carved into it, and the jaguar is wearing a crown.

Boots and I are going to need *your* help to get to the pyramid to see my *mami*. Who do we ask for help when we don't know which way to go? Yeah, the Map! Say "Map!"

Map says that we have to go across Emerald Canyon. Then we have to climb down the Steep Steps, and that's how we'll get to my *mami.*

¡Vámonos! Let's go!

Can you see Emerald Canyon? There it is! But it's so deep! How are we going to get across? Can you see something we can use to zip over the canyon?
Yeah! We can use the rope swing!

Wheeeee!

We made it over Emerald Canyon!

Uh-oh! Can you see Swiper? I think that sneaky fox wants to swipe our turquoise stone. We have to stop him. Quick! Say "Swiper, no swiping!"

Thanks for helping us stop Swiper. Where do we go next?
That's right – the Steep Steps!

Can you see the Steep Steps? There they are!

Wow, these steps are really steep! Let's hold on to the rail.

We have to climb down ten steps. Will you help us count?
¡Uno, dos, tres, cuatro, cinco, seis, siete, ocho, nueve, diez!

We made it down the Steep Steps! Good counting! And there's my *mami* at the pyramid.

Mami says the stone belongs at the Museum of Ancient Art. We can take it there right away. *¡Vámonos!* Let's go!

The museum director says we found an ancient treasure
- the missing piece from the stone jaguar's medallion!

We can put the stone back where it belongs.

We did it! We found and returned the stone. *¡Gracias!* Thanks for helping!